The Snowy Hill

by Karen Walberg • illustrated by John Bennett

Bear looks at the thermometer.

Bear gets a jacket.

3

He gets a snowboard.

Squirrel looks at the thermometer.

Squirrel gets a sweater.

She gets a sled.

Moose looks at the thermometer.

Moose gets boots.

He gets skis.

Bear goes up.

Squirrel and Moose go up.

Bear, Squirrel, and Moose
go down!